THE

GREATEST

CRIME

NEVER

COMMITTED

By: Cameron R. Higgason

CHAPTER

1

Have no fear of that voice inside your head you hear when you look at this piece of paper that has a bunch of letters perfectly arranged to form words and phrases, it's just me. But who is "me"? I am no one. I am just a thought, I'm a storyteller, an NPC or non-playable character. I am no main protagonist, rather I'm just an extra. Now throughout the journey of life, we are reminded just how short of a ride it can be and to enjoy every moment like it's our last. To seize every waking second and hold on as if our lives depended on it because for one of those seconds it does. That is how Danny lived his life whether he realized it or not. Personally, I don't think he did but I don't think he cared either just because that's how Danny was as a person. Danny Collins, the man who orchestrated the greatest crime never committed.

Danny was a kid who was dealt the wrong hand in life and played it accordingly. He didn't grow up with a close-knit family. His dad's parents lived on the other side of the country, and Danny's mother was born in some underground whorehouse. Where she never knew her father for her mother was the popular one in the house. The government came and took her away in a big raid and just like that she became an orphan, a property of the state, or at least for a moment in time until she would run away. They always managed to find her and bring her back, but once given the chance she was gone again. Eventually, the orphanage ceased to care and stopped looking for her. By then his mom had dropped out of the ninth grade. She ran away to be with Danny's father who promised to support her and the curly-haired baby in her stomach with his job as a construction worker. Then 1987 hit, the financial crisis left

Danny's father unemployed. But, he didn't let the pressure get the better of him, he did what every good Catholic does, he drank. His mom had a tendency to smoke while she was pregnant with Danny. She claimed the Menthol numbed the pain of carrying a 10 pound human inside of her womb. She would smoke even more during contractions, but it also happened to numb Danny's brain, so you could say he was screwed from the beginning. His father, who by the time Danny was born, was a full-time alcoholic drunk who would go on wild gambling sprees using money he didn't have and every time coming back with nothing to show for it but a deeper debt than before. He then would take out his frustrations on Danny's mom, they say the pen is mightier than the sword but to Danny and his mom, the pen didn't hold a candle to his father's fist. Silence in his household was reserved for when his dad was either gone or passed out drunk and when his mom was sleeping or "sleeping" on the ground after she would take the sucker punch from his dad so he wouldn't catch it. It got to the point where shouting was just as good as silence. Danny would go to school to learn vocabulary during the day then come home and learn "French" from that night's dispute. Danny would go back to school the next day and teach the other children what he learned the night before.

Throughout all the pain and abuse his father put both Danny and his mom through, Danny's mother stood by him. She really took the "till death do us part" vow literally, well until death came lurking. One night when Danny was in the living room watching cartoons while sitting on the green stained carpet, shouting and sobbing could be heard from the bedroom. The shouting was his dad. The sobbing was his mom, as usual, only this time a phrase never uttered before in the house rang through the halls,

"I'm leaving!" Danny's mom screamed.

Danny's drunk father did not approve of this idea or the newfound confidence in his mom. "You think you can leave me? You'll never be anything without me! I'm all you got." He shouts back as a boom can be heard coming from the bedroom they were both in.

While Danny's mom was packing she didn't see his father grab his .38 special from out of his nightstand. Lucky for her he was so drunk he was seeing three of her and too stupid to aim for the middle one. Quickly, Danny's mom grabbed him and headed for the car. Around the time they were halfway down the street, Danny turned to look back at his home where his dad stood in the doorframe of the entrance with his dingy white wife-beater shirt glued to his chest with beer sweat soaking through the cotton. Messy dirty blonde hair that looks like it hasn't been combed in weeks and his pistol still in hand. The only thing holding him up was the wall. The once sun-bleached house was lit up with red and blue lights. The last time Danny saw his dad was when he was getting loaded up in the back of a squad car. After a few months in general population within the prison, One of the mob's shot callers put a green light on Danny's dad, he didn't make it to the end of the day before someone shanked him while out on the yard. They stabbed him right in the back. The prison got a hold of Danny's mom and told her the news, not a single ounce in her could care. The news went in one ear and out the other, so much so she forgot to tell Danny about it. A week later was his funeral. It was an open casket as if that matters, no one bothered to show up to it. moral of the story, pay your debts or at least don't take out loans with the mob you know you can't afford to pay back.

For all the bad Danny's dad caused to the family, Danny never knew any better, he assumed all families were like this so to him his father was never a no-good alcoholic wife-beating bum like his mom described him, to Danny he was just "Dad" and seeing his dad get swarmed by the police was very traumatic for an already troubled mind. Danny would begin to act out at school. He would start fights, break things, one time he even sliced a teacher with safety scissors, sounds pretty safe. He was visiting the principal's office so much he started to refer to the principal as his second dad. It was fitting as he was always shouting at Danny, only Danny saw his second dad a lot more often than his biological dad.

Danny's mom found an apartment on the other side of town that they started renting. By renting I mean squatting. They were always so late for the rent that they were just early for the next month's bill. I'd like to say it was a nice apartment though. But it wasn't. The dust and cigarette smoke always seemed to fill the sunbeams that poured in through the windows. The kitchen had lightly stained white linoleum flooring.

Danny's mom has now accrued her fair share of jobs. Nothing fancy, she has just been through almost every fast food joint and grocery store in the town, but with car problems and unscheduled principal visits being ever so common, she found it hard to last more than a month anywhere she went. However now she works at the gas station right on the same corner of the street the apartment is on, which means car problems are no longer an issue. It seems Danny knew this as school visits seemed to have doubled since.

As Danny entered into middle school he discovered God's gift to earth, punk music! Danny would have the whole apartment complex shaking to bands like The Misfits, Dead Kennedys, and Black Flag. Like every good 13 year old who discovers music almost as violent as they are, he began to dress the part. Lucky for him holes came cheap in his clothes, nothing like having hand-me-downs as an only child. One day as he was leaving school and heading home, he walked past a section of the school and heard this heavy music playing, it almost lifted Danny off his feet as he tracked the source down like a Basset Hound. It was coming from under the bleachers on the football field. The people there were decked out in leather and chains and no two people had the same color of hair, finally people Danny can relate to. Danny would meet his new clique every day after school under the same bleachers where they would blare their musical choice of that day and all smoke Camel Reds Turkish Blend that one of the kids had stolen from his dad. Danny began to form a close bond with the ringleader of them all, his name was Curt. Curt also came from a troubled home and spent many nights sleeping under the very same bleachers that the group met at. He and Danny really connected for their love of the horror punk band Misfits and from there a brotherhood was formed. No longer was Curt sleeping under the bleachers. Instead, he would sleep over at Danny's house. Every day from then on out when the gang would all go their separate ways Danny and Curt would go back to the apartment, watch MTV and hang out till nightfall. This went on for several weeks until finally, Danny asked his mom if Curt could move in with them. Curt had become an unofficial member of the family and had been given chores he was in charge of and he never had any problems doing them but when the question came up about Curt officially moving in Danny's mom became hesitant. Would the landlord approve? Finally, after a bit of time, she agrees. I mean after all he hasn't given her a reason to be against it and they were already late on their rent as is, what's the worst thing that the landlord could do? Kick them out?

CHAPTER

2

A few years have passed, Curt and Danny have grown out of the old clique that they were in and now just stick with each other. Curt has grown comfortable with living with Danny and his mom. Out of the billions of people in the world all those three have are each other. Their holidays may not be glamorous. People may not be coming out in droves. But they are still just as grand as any other family. During Thanksgiving, they all three come together to make a big meal. On Christmas, they sit around a Charlie Brown Christmas tree and exchange gifts. One year Curt managed to save up enough to get Danny a nice leather jacket just like the kind some of his idols wore. From that day on Danny refused to take that thing off. On Ash Wednesday they would fast. By they, I mean Danny's mom as Danny and Curt would sneak out and go get burgers at a diner called Dukes. There they would shoot pool and grab a bite to eat. Danny loved their mushroom Swiss burger but, the best had to be their curly fries with a side of cheese dip. I wonder whatever happened to that place. Come Halloween Curt would always dress up as Doyle Wolfgang Von Frankenstein and Danny would go as Glenn Danzig. They were out for more of the tricks than they were for the treats.

Time seemed to have flown by, Danny Collins the little boy we all know and love had now entered into High School. He and Curt walked to their first day of high school, leather jackets and all. Danny wasn't much of an artist, but he was proud of the Misfits logo he painted on the back of his jacket. A chain hung off his black jeans. Holes filled the space that denim once laid on his knees.. Danny and Curt conversed the whole way to school while getting their first and last cigarette in before school started. They arrived on campus just in time to hear the first bell and watch all the other students get herded inside so as to not be late.

"Like cows going to slaughter." Curt joked as he went to pass Danny the cigarette.

But before Danny was able to have a full grip on the butt of the cigarette an old, translucent, wrinkled hand swiped it from Curt.

"There is absolutely no smoking on school grounds!" Said the teacher ,who was standing behind them, in a disciplinary voice.

She then turns to see Danny's artwork on his jacket.
"Misfits? Are you claiming to be some sort of misfit? Because I will not tolerate such things. You two better watch yourselves, I got a feeling we will be seeing more of each other, now get to class." The stern teacher ordered.

Danny and Curt did as they were told. As they made their way to the door Curt pulled out another cigarette, lit it, inhaled, and passed it over to Danny who also took a deep breath of it. He then extinguished what was left of the cigarette and placed it in one of the many pockets on his jacket for later. Curt and Danny had separate classes on opposite sides of the school. They parted ways and agreed they'd meet up at Duke's for lunch and shoot some pool.

Lunchtime rolls around and the two boys set off for Dukes. The place is packed for the lunch rush. It's clear they won't be getting food for a while. So they head to the back where the pool tables and arcade games are. As they approach the back, the clacking of pool balls being broken on the table can be heard. One of the local biker gangs seemed to have beat them to the table and had no intentions of being done by the time Curt and Danny had to be back at school. Cunning, Danny decides to converse with the bikers and eventually they warm up to him. Danny challenges one of the bikers to a game, he wagers twenty dollars that he can best the biker. Not looking to turn down a chance for some easy money the biker accepts. Curt pulls Danny aside,

"What are you doing?" Curt questions cautiously.

"I'm about to pay for our meals and then some."

The game starts off with Danny breaking the balls. He lines up his shot, pulls the pool stick back, and barely grazes the cue ball, sending it spinning like a top before bouncing off the triangle of balls barely moving anything. The bikers explode with laughter. Next, the biker takes his shot, easily sinking the first stripe in the corner pocket, then he sinks another, and another, only this time he accidentally sinks the cue ball with it. It's Danny's turn,

"So I'm the solid color ones right?" He asks as he takes aim at one of the balls.

Danny pulls back and with all his might, he nails the cue ball dead center, sending it rocketing toward the solid ball and sinking it. Again the bikers laugh uncontrollably,

"You just sank the eight ball! Run along now kid." The biker says in-between moments of laughter.

Curt looks at Danny with slight frustration for gambling away their lunch money and slightly embarrassed for Danny not knowing the rules of the game before betting.

"Double or nothing." Is heard slicing through the laughter and then the place gets silent.

"I said double or nothing." Danny says again.

The biker in disbelief of Danny's stupidity is quick to agree,

"easiest forty bucks I've made in a while."

Danny gathers the pool balls and racks them, this time the biker breaks.

With ease, he shoots the cue ball into the rest of the balls, and one by one they ricochet off the walls of the table but none find a home in the pockets. Danny lines up for his shot,

"To avoid what happened last time, I'm gonna be stripes."

He hits the ball sinking the nine-ball, then the ten ball, next the eleven ball, and he continues without missing a beat. Eventually, he sinks every single stripe ball and he does it in order. He is set for an easy shot at the eight to win and without any problems or obstacles he pockets the eight ball and takes the money and the boys leave the restaurant. The only problem is the bikers followed them. With anger from just being scammed and made to look like a fool in front of his entire gang, the biker sends a haymaker into the back of Danny's head sending him falling to the ground and out into the parking lot. A barrage of kicks and punches comes raining down on Danny by the gang. Curt is useless against five guys, so he wanders over to the line of motorcycles and one good push sends the bikes falling like dominoes stopping bikers beat down on Danny long enough for him to get up. Now the bikers are ready to take out Curt as well. So with Danny up and the bikes out of commission they ran as fast as their legs and tar-filled smoker lungs would allow them. However, they had no plans of going back to school. They were over that place. After all, learning is for idiots. Instead they opted to run back to the apartment and lick their wounds. When they got home Danny's mom was on her lunch as well and she didn't need to look too hard to see the bruises that were already forming on her son and the blood coming from his fat lip along with a possible broken nose.

"What happened to you?" Asked his shocked mom.

"I fell." Danny replied knowing full well snitches get stitches, ironically he was going to need stitches regardless. When Danny's mom went to the medicine cabinet to get the hydrogen peroxide, Danny began to flash his forty dollars to Curt in a very proud manner as if his plan had worked flawlessly.

CHAPTER

3

A week has passed since the pool hall brawl with the bikers and Danny's face is starting to look back to normal. Curt took this as the perfect time to let Danny in on a secret. One day Danny was hanging out in his room when Curt came storming in with his jacket on. He was obviously hiding something judging by his suspicious behavior.

"Dude you are not going to believe what I have for us!" Curt said in a very ecstatic voice.

Curt reaches into his pocket and pulls out a pipe.

"What's that for?" Asked Danny.

"Weed, it's for weed." Replied Curt with a hint of sarcasm in his voice.

"I know that part moron but I mean why do you have it? We don't have anything to use it with." Reiterated Danny.

That was when Curt opened his jacket with a big smile on his face, the kind of smile you have when you know something the other person doesn't, and he pulls out a brick of weed.

"Where did you get all of that?" Asked Danny with amazement.

"I stole it!" Answered Curt with excitement.

"Stole it from who?" Danny questioned.

"Those bikers, man. Remember when I kicked over the bikes? Well it was in one of their saddlebags and it fell out and I snagged it before we left. I was thinking we could sell the majority of it and make a little side money while also keeping some for ourselves because you know, taxes." Said Curt.

Danny and Curt then load up the pipe and take turns passing it back and forth to each other till they were both stoned like a gravel road. Danny feels the munchies beginning to set in. So he trudges through the dense smoke, makes it to the door and stumbles down the stairs to the kitchen. He opens the fridge and rifles through the selection of food before in the back he sees the thing that is sure to hit the spot but right as he goes to grab it a voice could be heard behind him, it was his mom, as she began to speak it spooked Danny enough where he jumped knocking stuff around in the fridge.

"Danny I have to go to work now, be good and can you please clea..." Danny's mom announced as Danny stared at her with a thousand yard stare, you know that stare where it's like they are looking through you, as he swayed softly back and forth watching his mom's lips move but so caught up within his own inner monologue that he had lost the sense of hearing.

"...and finish the dishes." She ended on just in time for Danny's hearing to come back.

"Right mom, you got it" Danny replied before reaching back in the fridge grabbing what seemed like the holy grail to him and running back to his room.

"Dude where'd you go?" asked Curt.

"I wanted a Pepsi." Danny answered while pointing to the can in Danny's hand. This caused them to both burst out in laughter.

The next day they get to school on their best behavior. Having a brick of marijuana in your backpack tends to bring the best out of even the most troublesome of people. Danny and Curt knew exactly how they would go about selling their stolen product. First they would start with the lowlifes and the hopeless kids, the ones that have no future and are just there to make sure we don't breathe up all the oxygen for ourselves. Yeah, those kids are first on the list. Next on the list are the meatheads, the kids who are only in high school because they can throw a ball far. Those morons are where the money is because they buy in bulk for all their game day bangers. They are typically followed by the girls who every adult thinks is a classy Christian girl. Oh but if they only knew what really takes place when they aren't around, those red marks on her knees aren't from praying to the All Mighty like she said. Anyways, it doesn't take long for word to spread and suddenly Danny and Curt are racking in tons of money with their overpriced devil's lettuce. It seems all is finally right in the world, the students are happy, Danny is making tons of money and by doing so helping his mom pay off some of the debt she has accrued. Danny's mom wants to ask where he came up with the money but times are tough and ignorance is bliss. Within less than two weeks Danny had sold all of the weed. Too bad he was now hooked. Not on weed, but rather on selling it.

Every time they had to turn a potential customer away due to lack of inventory, their popularity seemed to diminish. Ah, the sweet feeling of being used. Danny knew they needed to find more product but had no idea who to talk to about getting more. The only two people in the town that were dealing were Danny and the bikers Curt stole from and something told Danny they weren't keen on making any business deals with them. So it seemed their reign of terror was finished, ending as swiftly as it began. Danny started to reacclimate to his old way of living but Curt was not prepared to go back. Au Contraire mon frère, Curt was looking at the bigger picture. Danny wakes up for school to find Curt missing but a letter is left in his place "Danny, I got an idea. See you after school." Not thinking anything about it Danny gets ready to go to school. Once school is over Danny starts his walk home following his usual route when suddenly he is pulled into an alley by his jacket. Before Danny knows what is going on he sees a black metal object in his face.

"Gimme your money!" The voice says. By now, Danny realized the object is in fact a gun. Before Danny can say anything the voice begins to laugh.

"Oh you should have seen the look on your face!" says Curt.

"Dude, you could have killed me! Where did you get a gun!" Says a freaked out Danny.

"Relax you fairy, it's not loaded. I got the bullets in my pocket. I traded my last remaining buds of weed to that homeless vet for this gun and a couple of bullets, it's our next big money maker." Curt replies.

"Next big money maker, what are you talking about?" Asked Danny.

"Look, you don't think it took me nine hours to get this, do you? While you were in class I was staking out the gas station down the street." Answered Curt.

"You are wanting to rob the gas station?" Asked Danny with a worried look on his face.

"Precisely Dannyboy, look it's simple around 10:30am the place is all but empty besides the employee. All we have to do is go in there and flash a gun around and they will give us the money, trust me no one is willing to get shot over money that's not theirs." Curt says in a voice as if he had thought the whole thing through.
"So me and you, tomorrow, ditching school for our first day of our new job." Curt says happily.

CHAPTER

4

Today is the day, the day Danny and Curt take that next big leap in the criminal world. Danny had trouble sleeping last night as thoughts flooded his brain of everything that could go wrong. Although Curt seems confident enough in his plan, honestly how great could his plan really be after watching a store for just one day. But it all doesn't matter now, it was too late to back out. Danny and Curt get dressed in clothes they typically didn't wear, Danny didn't even wear his leather jacket so as to not give away their identity. The two boys hung around the house for a couple of hours before they started their walk to school only to make a detour towards the gas station. Danny checks his watch that reads 9:59 am. Butterflies fill Danny's stomach, deep down he hopes that for whatever reason the store is actually busy today at 10:30 so he will have room to convince Curt to call off the robbery. Anxiety quickly takes control of Danny as his leg twitches uncontrollably. Curt on the other hand looked calm and collected like a lion stalking the gazelle, he was laser-focused and eager to get going. Danny checks his watch again, now it reads 10:15. Suddenly, a cop car pulls into the parking lot. Danny takes a breath of relief as he knows that Curt is smart enough to not to try a robbery now that the cop is there. It's now 10:20 am and the cop walks out of the store, enters his vehicle, and sits in the parking lot filling out paperwork. Curt's face drops as the clock winds down, getting closer to that golden period for the heist that can't be done with a police officer sitting right at the front door. Then a call comes over the radio and the car backs up, turns on the sirens, and speeds down the road. Danny checks his watch one last time, it's 10:29 am, and Curt's smile returns along with Danny's butterflies. Curt begins to walk across the street and onto the empty parking lot. He and Danny enter the store and the clerk greets them as the chimes from the door still ring. They walk back to the cooler area where the beer is located and wander around trying to not act suspicious. Curt takes some beef jerky and carries it to the cashier. The cashier scans it and Curt hands him the money. Right when the cashier opens the register to put the money in he is met with Curt's pistol being pointed at him. With no hesitation, the cashier throws up his hands and Curt directs him to step out from behind the register. Once he is away, Danny slides over and begins to empty out the cash. Once it's all gone Curt tells the cashier to close his eyes and count to twenty and the boys dart out of the store. Danny was amazed that it was a success. Still high on the adrenaline, he reaches into his pockets to count how much money they made. They start with the big bills and work their way down till there is nothing left. Overjoyed, they come to the grand total of seven hundred fifty dollars. Just like that, the boys found their new hobby. Without allowing the rush to wash away, Curt is already thinking of new places to hit up. Danny finds this attitude alarming and dangerous because Curt isn't even thinking of logical places. Instead he has thrown out ideas like robbing the library. To Curt, it wasn't about the money as much as it was for the feeling. Danny continues to brush Curt's list of places aside as to not encourage him, Danny really just wanted to relish in the moment they were in and just be happy they weren't caught. They finally get home and walk in to find Danny's mom waiting for them with a stern look of disappointment on her face.

"I know what you two did today!" She said with anger in her voice. The boys look shocked and Danny starts to get nervous, how will he explain the robbery to his mom?

"You do?" Danny asked with a shaken voice.

"Yeah I do, did you really think you two could skip school and the school wouldn't call me?" Said his mom. At this point, all of Danny's fears have subsided, he could tell his mom wasn't happy about them skipping school but as long as that's all she knows then Danny was happy. Danny and Curt were sent to their room as punishment for playing hooky that day but still, they felt euphoric over getting away with the real bad thing.

The next morning, Danny's mom drives the boys to school to make sure they find their way there, she waits out in her Station Wagon and doesn't leave till the boys walk through the school doors. At lunch that day Curt and Danny sit at their usual table. While Danny and Curt were eating, Curt continued on about how they needed to find their next target. Just then three cheerleaders walk by, Curt began eavesdropping on their conversation about how one of the football players was throwing a party but it had since been canceled since he failed his drug test and on top of his football suspension his parents grounded him. You can't help but think Curt and Danny had a role in that drug test being failed. Curt would quickly mosey his way over to them. With a smile fit for a politician's face, Curt tells the three young ladies that he is in fact going to be throwing a massive party that weekend. The girls were skeptical.

"Do you even have a house?" One asked with a snobby voice.

"Of course, I just bought one on the Northside of town." Curt replied.

"You bought a house?" Another girl asked.

"Yep, it's all mine. If you don't believe me then that's fine. Just stop by Saturday and see for yourself, it's the house with the sold sign in the front yard." Curt replied.

And like a knight to a damsel in distress, Curt had saved the day. Curt with a new pep in his step, struts back over to Danny.

"Looks like we are throwing a house party this weekend." Curt tells Danny. Confused, Danny looks at Curt,

"how? My mom won't let us have a party in that little apartment." Asked Danny.

"We will kill two birds with one stone." Replied Curt. Just then the bell rings and lunch is over.

"Trust me." Is the last thing Curt says before heading off in the opposite direction from Danny.

CHAPTER
5

Curt and Danny return home from school. In Danny's bedroom, which at this point seems to be the planning room for their mischief, Danny asked Curt what his plan was to kill two birds with one stone. Curt explains the interaction he had with the group of girls. He explains that not only is this a prime opportunity to impress some girls, but also how it sets up a perfect opportunity for another robbery only this time a house instead of a business.

"What we will do is go up to the northside of town and go door to door knocking and asking if anyone would be interested in having their lawns cut on the weekend." Curt explains. Danny, not quite getting the full scope of the idea, figures Curt knows what he is doing seeing as how seamless the last robbery went. So with no more questions, Danny is now in on this plan, and just like that they head off for the Northside of town. Once they arrive on this pristine road filled with cookie-cutter two-story houses with multi-car garages, they each take turns going door to door to each house on the street trying to pitch this shell landscape company of Curt's to whoever would listen. The more they were rejected the more Danny started to catch on to the small details that Curt had thought of. He knew this was the rich part of town so the large majority already have gardeners, this would prevent them from having anyone coming to look for them when they didn't cut the lawn. Finally, after what seems like an hour of knocking and getting rejected, Danny comes to a bluish-gray house with white trim and a bricked driveway. Danny approaches the door and grabs a hold of the brass door knocker. A heavier set man dressed in a business shirt answers the door. Danny goes on to tell him about how they are two young entrepreneurs looking to make some side money on the weekends when they aren't busy with their schooling and was wondering if this fine gentleman would be interested in his lawn being immaculately cut that weekend. The man, who clearly didn't have time for the charade, quickly rejected Danny. He goes on to explain that as much as he would love to support a local business he wouldn't be home that particular weekend because he and his family were going out of town and then quickly shut the door. Finally, it all clicked, the whole plan Curt had created made sense now. Danny returned to Curt who was waiting for him on the sidewalk.

"This is the house." Danny said.

"Great, now we need to head to the hardware store and get a sign." Replied Curt.

The weekend quickly rolls around and Curt and Danny get dressed in their finest attires and make their way to a nearby liquor store, this store never had a shortage of homeless drunks. If Danny didn't watch his dad get arrested he would think one of them was his father. With a quick bribery of booze they pay one of the homeless to buy them alcohol, they hand him the money and watch him stumble into the store. It's not a long wait before he comes stumbling back out with a couple of black bags in one hand and a bottle of whiskey in the other. He hands them the black bags and then heads off to find a comfy pile of trash to down his adult beverage and pass out on. The boys journey off to "Curt's" house to begin setting up. As they round their way to the street, they make it just in time to see the man and his wife packing the last bit of their stuff into their sleek Bentley, and their daughter hops in the back and they take off. Curt waits to see the taillights vanish over the hill and then he goes into action. He is quick to stake down the "For Sale" sign that they got at the hardware store and with a hard smack he slaps a big red "sold" sticker over the sign. The boys then make their way to the front door only to discover it is locked. Curt flips up the welcome mat, grabs the key, and unlocks the door.

"How did you know that was there?" Asked Danny.

"Where do you keep your spare key?" Answered Curt with a question.

"Under the welcome ma..." Danny began to reply before shutting up. They walk in to get a good feel of the place and take mental pictures of the placement of every single object in the house. Once they enter the kitchen Danny starts unpacking the black bags onto the counter. Afterward, they had time to relax and wait a little bit before everyone showed up. Right as the sun began to set all of the people Curt had told about the party started to show up.

Before long there were thirty people at the party which only went on to make the whole thing seem legit when the three girls arrived. Astonished by what they saw, they went up to Curt to compliment him on what they believed to be his house. It didn't take long for the alcohol to not be enough and some of the attendees were asking Curt for some more hardcore stuff. Curt, being a good host, agreed and went up the stairs to try to find anything to satisfy his crowd. He went into the master bedroom thinking they would have something in their nightstands. He was right, they did have stuff in their nightstands, just no drugs. Curt eagerly called for Danny to come check out what he had found. Danny excuses himself from the conversation he was invested in and goes upstairs. Danny enters the master bedroom where Curt was calling him from.

"Yeah Curt!" Danny called out as he looked around unable to see Curt. "Curt?" Danny asked as he searched for him. As Danny walks deeper into the room the bedroom door is kicked shut and this karate squeal is heard coming from behind him as Danny gets whipped in the back of the head. He turns around to see Curt laughing hysterically while waving a leather flogger around like it's nunchucks and wearing a gimp mask with the mouth unzipped. Danny sees this and has no choice but to no longer be mad and start laughing with Curt.

"Where did you find that?" Danny asks in between laughs.

"I was looking for drugs when I found it in the nightstands. Check out the photos I found with it." Curt answers while trying to pull his head out of the mask like a baby being born. Danny goes over to the nightstand and looks in to find Polaroid photos of a big gutted man wearing the mask and underwear on all fours along with what we can only assume to be his wife with the flogger in her hand. Seems this suburban Americana family has some secrets. Danny takes the photos and puts them in the inside pocket of his jacket and goes back downstairs. Curt returns to his quest of looking for anything that can send his houseguest to the moon. He goes on to check the bathroom and to his success, he finds several bottles of pills. He takes it downstairs to the party and is met with cheers. He drops the pills into a big bowl and pours in the alcohol to be served to all the people.

Curt feels like he runs the world but in an instant, his kingdom falls. Red and blue lights flash from outside. "Cops!" Someone screams, the one word that can be heard over even the loudest of music. Quickly, everyone begins to scatter and run in all directions. Curt and Danny both were too slow and they got caught and cuffed. They are taken in with the charges of breaking and entering and drugs. Not something that makes them look like saints by any means. Once booked they were given their one phone call. Danny reluctantly called his mom to tell her he needed her to come bail him and Curt out of jail. Danny's mom could be heard screaming through the phone before Danny shamefully thanked her for her coming and hanging up. One of the cops asked Curt if he was ready to make a phone call to which Curt replied

"He just called the only person I could call and she doesn't seem like she wants to talk."

CHAPTER

6

After what seems like an eternity of waiting, Danny's mom arrives at the police station where both Danny and Curt are being held in a small cell in the back. Danny was stricken with anxiety as he sat in the cold cell unsure of how his mom would react once she got there. One thing he was sure about is that no mother ever acts happy when they have to drive late at night to bail their teenage son out of jail. The anxiety seemed to disappear and in its place formed the emotion of dread when he peered out in between the bars and saw his mom talking to the officer. Danny was unable to hear the conversation but knew he was in for a long car ride home because periodically through the hand gestures of the officer, Danny's mom would glance over at him with a scorned look of disappointment painting her face. Eventually, the officer and Danny's mom walk over to the cell. The officer pulls out the keys and unlocks the sliding door and as the metal door bangs at the end of its track the officer tells the boys, "you are free to go." Danny and Curt walk out past the officer and over to Danny's mom, Danny had his head buried into his shoulder like he was expecting to get hit, instead, Danny's mom just ordered the boys to get in the car.

It was an excruciatingly long and silent car ride home. No words were spoken and no song played over the radio. This only added to Danny's fear. He couldn't help but wonder why he wasn't being yelled at right now. The car whips around and the headlights shine onto the steps of the sleeping apartment complex before the car is shut off returning the building back into the peaceful darkness. Everyone gets out of the car and in no rhythmic timing, the car doors shut one by one. It continues to be silent as they walk up the concrete steps they can hear the echoes of their steps through the metal pipe that makes up the framing of the stairs. Danny's mom unlocks the door to the apartment and flips on the light while simultaneously dropping her purse to the ground. The boys tried their best to sneak off to bed to try to avoid the inevitable lecture but to their demise, they are stopped right before they are about to leave the living room and be in the clear.

"How could you be so stupid?" Danny's mom asked while trying her best to swallow the rage.

"...and of all the houses to do this to you, pick the mayor's house. I'm honestly at a loss of words over this. Just go to your room and enjoy the remaining time you have not in jail Danny."

And so with their heads bent down in defeat, they head off to their rooms. Sleep didn't come easy for either of the boys. They were both still pretty shaken up from getting arrested and now the impending doom of being sentenced. Eventually, they manage to get a couple of hours of sleep. The boys get up and get dressed. Right before they leave though, Danny picks up his leather jacket and hears something coming from his pocket. He reaches in and pulls out the photos he had taken from the mayor's nightstand and the feeling of doom is gone and the feeling of hope is born. Danny can't wipe the smile off his face as he now knows he is not going to jail.

The boys head out the door and make their way over to the mayor's house where the mayor and his family are back home after their vacation was cut short by the house party. Danny and Curt walk up to the lawn that is still littered with trash and they make their way to the door and knock on it, the mayor answers the door and can't believe what he sees,

"Haven't you two done enough, or do I have to call the cops and add to the list of charges?" Asked the mayor.

"Actually I think you should call the cops and tell them to lower the list of charges, say to zero." Danny says with confidence.

"Yeah, right, now you are just wasting my time. Get out of here kids." The mayor replied while shutting the door. Danny catches the door from closing all the way

"I really think you should rethink your decision on those charges there Mr.Mayor. It would be political suicide should these get leaked to the wrong people." Danny says while showing the photos. Anger and astonishment came over the mayor,

"First you break into my house, destroy it, and now you are blackmailing me? Fine, consider the charges dropped as long as I never see you two again! Happy?" Says the mayor.

"Very!" Replies Danny and both boys walk away with a newfound look on life. Later on that night the phone rings and Danny's mom answers, nothing but a series of uh huhs can be heard. Finally his mom says goodbye, and the phone is heard clicking as she hangs up.

"Well that was the police station, it would seem the mayor had a change of heart and decided to not press charges." Danny's mom announces, she continues"now either the mayor is feeling stupidly generous or you two did something, but to be honest I don't want to know, just count yourselves lucky this time, and remember everyone's luck runs out eventually."

The next morning the boys are radiating joy. They feel as though they have escaped death. They wake up before they are needed to wake up, they are dressed and ready and practically skipping out the door. They make it to school, not late this time. They even had time before the first bell to congregate in the cafeteria. There in the cafeteria, a kid named Eugene approached Danny. Eugene was not the best looking, or the most fun to be around, not really funny, was more concerned about grades, nerd, Eugene was a nerd to put it plain and simple. Anyways Eugene searched out Danny in hopes of scoring some weed. Danny quickly brushed him off. Some dork trying to get weed seemed like a narc move and besides that Danny didn't have any for public use. Eugene went on to explain he was at the house party of horror and saw his crush there, he was hoping to get some marijuana to impress her and show that he can be bad sometimes, he even offered to pay Danny with Misfits tickets. Eugene did his homework on Danny and knew the way to his heart. Eugene's story pulled at Danny's heartstrings, mainly the part about paying with concert tickets, so he agreed to the love-struck dweeb's terms and they went to Danny's locker and Eugene gave him the tickets and Danny gave him one bud from his personal stash and just like that they went their separate ways. About two class periods go by and Danny is called to the office. When he entered the office the secretary buzzed the principal to let him know Danny was there. Danny was quickly escorted into the principal's office where the principal, superintendent, and Eugene were sitting down. Seems when Eugene went to try to win some love he forgot to check his surroundings, a teacher quickly saw the weed, and Eugene was rushed to the principal's office. I wish I could tell you Eugene was a tough nut to crack, I wish I could tell you that they had to put him through intense Chinese torture to get him to talk, I wish they would have waterboarded him. Instead, he was ratting out Danny's whole operation before he even made it to the office. He could have snitched faster if it weren't for the hyperventilating and stream of tears coming off his face. Not long after Danny makes it to the Office, Curt walks in. It seems their luck had finally run out. Danny's mother was called to come pick up the two boys. Without much thought, they were quickly expelled from school.

CHAPTER

7

Though only a few blocks away, the silence in the car made it feel like time came to a halt as Danny's mother white knuckles the steering wheel with pure anger over her son but no words are spoken. It seems like only yesterday this same car ride was being taken. A real sense of Deja Vu. Once inside the house, the door slamming shut behind them acted as the play button ending the silence. All Danny can do is stand there shoulder to shoulder with Curt as Danny's mom unloads on them. This should have had a lot more effect on the two than what it actually did, the two boys were barely even listening with the thought of the upcoming Misfits concert flooding their minds. Eventually, though the background noise of Danny's mom screaming in their faces begins to end and their ears become more adjusted to reality with Danny's mom giving the sternest face to them, and as funny as her face might have looked to them they dared not to laugh.

"Did you not hear me? I said go to your room!" Danny's mom yells as she points in the general direction of the boys' room.

Danny, with a lack of care about the expulsion, falls down onto his worn-out spring mattress. Curt is thrilled to be expelled from school, he sees it as a dream come true. He had no ambitions to do anything with an education and now he has nothing but time for planning new jobs. But jobs are the last thing on his mind with the concert quickly approaching. Only a few more hours till nightfall and the show will be starting.

Confined to their room the boys watch the sun go down and the moon go up. Knowing that Danny's mom won't be checking on them they sneak out through the window decked out in leather and face paint and head off to the show. The venue looks like a scene from The Night of the Living Dead as ghoulish creatures wander around waiting for the openers to finish their last song. The security guard working the door takes the boys' tickets and they are allowed in. They don't waste their time at any of the vendors considering it's not like they had any money to spend at them anyways so they rush to find their spots and scope out any way to get closer. The house lights dim as the stage lights turn on in colorful fashion. Up on the stage, legendary shadows approach their corresponding instruments and with a thunderous roar the show starts.

It does not take long for a moshpit to form and Danny and Curt are quick to join, rushing into the chaotic circle of flying bodies. Curt is snatched up and separated from Danny. Danny is feeling the music as he flails around. Not paying attention, he catches a fist into the nose causing him to see stars. An apologetic voice embraces Danny as the two leave to the edge of the pit. Once Danny comes back to his senses he sees the culprit of the brutal hit is this punk rock girl.

"I am so sorry!" she says.

"Ah don't worry about it. What's your name?" Danny asks.

She replies, "Sheena." Danny could feel there was a connection between him and Sheena and with Curt gone he decides to tag along with her for the remainder of the show and that's what they did. As they were dancing in the sea of people Curt would occasionally stop by to express how amazing the show was before being swept back up by a human riptide.

With the last drumbeat echoing throughout Danny's skull, the concert was officially over, and as far as Danny was concerned it was well worth the expulsion from his school. I mean a high school diploma is only temporary but the Misfits, the Misfits are forever.

The house lights turn back on and like a pack of cockroaches, the zombies creep their way for the doors funneling out of the venue and into the quite empty dark streets lit only by the orange tint of the street lights, the smell of cigarette smoke quickly fills the troposphere. Danny easily manages to bum a cigarette off a nearby fiend and he lights it and passes it over to Sheena. For the remainder of that cigarette, Danny and Sheena hang outside the venue on the cold sidewalk filling each other in on their lives. Danny tells Sheena the story of his dad and how he is hopeful that prison will change his father and that when he gets out maybe they will be able to reconcile. Sheena goes on to beat him in the "who had a worse upbringing" competition as she confides in Danny that she never even knew her father and it only got worse from there.

She goes on to tell how at a young age her mother developed cancer. Single mom stuck in the midwest, she couldn't afford the treatments and so she withered away. Sheena goes on to explain that on the day of her mother's death the State came but refusing to go into an orphanage she ran away before the first shovel full of dirt hit her mother's hand-me-down casket. Ever since then she has been doing anything it took to make it on her own. Danny was taken back by this, the only person who ever compared to Danny's struggles was that of Curt but at least they could lean on Danny's mother to provide.

"If you are a runaway, where do you live?" Danny asked.

With a puff off the cigarette, she goes on to tell of how she found an apartment and managed to fake her age. After that, the cigarette was all but gone. Sheena took some ash from the end of the butt and crudely wrote her number onto Danny's arm and strutted off disappearing like a phantom into the night.

Danny, for once, had a thing to look forward to when he got home. The whole walk home he was going over the number so as to not forget should something happen to the marking. Lucky for him though he safely makes it home with his arm and with Sheena's number still intact. He climbs back up into the window of his bedroom, unlocks the door, and goes into the kitchen where the landline phone is hanging on the wall. He shuffles through the junk drawer that is filled with everything that doesn't have a place to go, scrounging through the tape, thimbles, overdue bills, thread, till eventually, he finds a pen. With no time to find a piece of paper Danny transfers the numbers from his arm and scribes them onto the wall next to the phone and heads off to bed once again.

CHAPTER

8

Danny was pretty smart for someone who just recently got kicked out of high school. He didn't want to appear desperate and he knew the rule to this was to wait three days before that first call and even though as agonizing as it was Danny stuck it out and waited three days. But he was waiting by the phone for the final hour. Once the hour was up the phone was in his hand and his fingers dialing the numbers in the order the wall said. With every ring from the phone the knot in his stomach tightens till finally, he hears the click of the receiver as the other end of the line is picked up and the rings are replaced with a soft and simple "hello?" and with that, the knot in his stomach loosens and he leans himself against the wall as they get lost in conversation. Hours went by so quickly. Just as the conversation felt like it was getting to something deeper Danny's mom comes home from work and parents him to get off the phone and quit running up the phone bill. So Danny had to say his goodbyes and hang up the phone.

Now that Danny has all day to spend at home he dedicated most of his time to talking to Sheena on the phone. He begins to learn his mom's work schedule so he can be off the phone thirty minutes before she comes home so he doesn't have to hear her rant and rave about the bills every day. He'd rather only have to hear it once a month when the bill itself showed up at the doorstep.

One day Danny calls Sheena and she begins to tell him all about a flier she saw. It was for the yearly fair that comes to town and without her having to say it while still hinting at it she coursed Danny into asking her if she would like to go to the fair with him. Before he was done asking the question she had already agreed to go. This would be their first official date.

The night of the fair arrives,
Danny has his leather jacket on that he
always wears, a ratted-up band shirt,
jeans with only a minimal amount of
holes in them, and his black boots.
Sheena comes in fishnet stockings and
dark-colored makeup. They pay their
way in and go through the rotating gate.
The air smells of sweat and funnel cakes,
the same repetitive jingle plays and
flashing lights of all colors can be seen
trying to lure every kid to their ride.
Sheena and Danny walk around the
fairground playing some of the scams
that they call games. Danny gets her a
stuffed animal and they go to a booth
and get some food to eat before going to
some other attractions. Once they feel
they have done everything they have set
out to do they decide to leave the fair.
Though neither of them wish to call it a
night and so they head off to find a clear
and quiet place to watch the stars.
Danny thinks he knows the perfect place

that is more their scene and so the two head off with Danny leading the way. When they reach the spot they find a place to lay down in the field and begin to stargaze and make small talk and pointing out shooting stars as they fly across the clear night sky until the night is abruptly interrupted when a blinding light is shined in the face of Danny followed by a voice of

"What are you two doing here?"

Danny, trying to cover his face from the light, responds,

"Just trying to look at the stars."

"Well not here you're not!" the voice replies.

"Why not?" asked Danny.

"Look around, you're in a cemetery, find somewhere else!"

As Danny and Sheena start to stand up they see the voice is owned by a police officer who does not look like he has a sense of humor and so they comply and the officer escorts them back to the gates of the graveyard where his patrol car was parked with no lights on. Danny and Sheena stand by the gate and watch the officer get in the car and drive away. Once they see the taillights vanish over the hill, they can't help but burst out laughing.

"Well since stargazing is no longer an option, wanna go get ice cream?" asked Danny. Sheena agrees and so they hold hands and walk down the road still giggling about getting kicked out of a cemetery. They barely make it to the ice cream parlor in time to get two sundaes. About halfway through their sundaes a waitress comes over to their booth and informs them that they have to close the place up. So they get up and take their glasses with them when the waitress isn't looking. Sheena mentions that her apartment is not too far and invites Danny over to finish the night. They finish their sundaes and Danny is the first to throw his glass breaking it on the ground. With a smirk, Sheena soon does the same.

Only a few blocks away and they arrive at a brick building. It seemed every apartment had some type of different commotion going on within it whether it was loud Spanish music, a married couple that should have gotten a divorce five years ago yelling at each other, or the consistent pounding on the wall. Sheena lived on the third floor and the elevator was not to be trusted so they made the venture up the stairs. Upon arrival a letter was taped to the door. Before Danny notices it, Sheena rips it off and folds it up into a tiny square before unlocking the door. Once inside, Danny takes in the scene. The apartment seemed to be falling apart. The green wallpaper had been peeled in certain spots, the blinds were bent in every direction, the wooden floorboards creaked with every step, duct tape could be seen covering the peephole on the

door as well as three different types of
locks were on the door. All in all, it
wasn't that bad of a place for a runaway.
Sheena didn't have much as far as
furniture. All the living room had was a
lamp sitting on the floor, a fabric couch,
a coffee table with cigarette ashes on it,
and an old record player with a milk
crate of records. She would go over to
turn on the lamp to barely light up the
living room and then go over to the milk
crate of records and pull out a Type O
Negative album and begin to play it,
balancing quarters on the needle so the
record wouldn't skip. As the methodical
melodies filled the room both Sheena
and Danny would slowly begin to drift
asleep sitting on the couch.

CHAPTER

9

Waking up in a daze, Danny looks around the unfamiliar house while rubbing his eyes. The sound of the record spinning but the music had stopped playing hours ago seemed to distort the half-sleeping Danny from being able to fully think. He looks to his side and sees a still sleeping Sheena. He slowly stands up and tries to not disturb her. He stumbles through the illuminating light coming from outside revealing all the dust in the air. He finds his way to the bathroom and closes the door. After going to the bathroom, Danny takes the time to splash some water in his face to wake himself up a bit more. Once he opens his eyes from the water he catches sight of a syringe, surgical tube, spoon, lighter, a small bag containing a white substance. Danny knew right away what it was and it woke him up faster than the water did. He yelled for Sheena from the bathroom. Sheena is shaken awake at the sound of

Danny yelling. She hurries to the bathroom expecting an emergency and instead gets Danny acting as if he was Nancy Reagan telling her to "just say no". Sheena is at a loss of words for this guy she just met to be dishing out disrespect as if he knew what was best for her in her own home. The two began to scream and yell, Danny yelling over the sudden realization his newly titled girlfriend is a meth addict, and Sheena was yelling because she had already ran away from one set of parents and was not out looking for any more of them. She grabs Danny and pushes him out of the bathroom and locks herself in. Danny begins to bang on the door yelling for her to open up. Sheena can be heard hyperventilating as she tries to yell back for him to leave. Eventually either they both got exhausted or both fed up with fighting that they sat in silence. Danny sitting up against the door on one side and Sheena sitting on the opposite side of the door. Danny is the first to speak,

"I just don't get why you would need to do that." he says through the door.

Sheena reluctantly answers his rhetorical question with "you wouldn't understand."

Danny pleads with her to just give him a good reason, finally with a sigh Sheena begins to open up. She explains that she lied about her father and that she regrettably does know her father, only her mother really did die and she ran away because her father had a habit of making forceful unwanted advances on Sheena. So it was either be molested till she was eighteen or run away from home. The part about her mother was true though. Danny was taken back by this. He was all for weed but never could imagine a good reason to get into anything as hardcore as meth but if there ever was a reason she seemed to have one he could not seem to argue with. Then the door unlocked and she came out with her eyes still red and her cheeks still flushed from sobbing. Danny no longer wanted to push the topic so he just pleaded with her to try and quit the addiction.

Danny spends the rest of the day with Sheena. Come nightfall, Sheena and Danny begin to walk back to Danny's house. Danny is going through in his head what he will tell his mom when he gets back since he never told her he would be gone all night. All he can do is hope she didn't notice. They decide to try to cut down an alleyway to shave off a few blocks. They are making good time going down the alley walking past all the hobos and crackheads of the town till they get about midway down one alleyway and then everything would go black for Danny. When he comes to, the back of his head is in a lot of pain, and Sheena screaming does not help.

Danny can't figure out what is wrong with his vision, why is everything sideways? Then he realized he was laying on the pavement and he felt an aggressive hand grip his shoulder, Danny was still too paralyzed to put up any fight. The hand rolls him over, now Danny can see it is the bikers from Duke's. Seems they have not forgotten. He sees Sheena not putting up much of a fight while two leather vest-wearing thugs restrain her. The leader of the gang stands over Danny with a loose board in his hand.

"You are lucky we need you alive to tell Curt we are coming for him, now get out of here and if we see you again you'll be dead."

The biker leader steps over Danny and his two goons release Sheena and walk away. Sheena runs to Danny's aid and helps him up. She is wondering the most obvious question anyone would ask in her shoes,

"Who were those guys?"

Danny, now on his feet, would have to go on to explain how he and Curt stole weed from them a while back in order to sell it to make some quick cash but ever since they sold it all, they have had to resort to other means of making money. This piques Sheena's curiosity,

"Now what are you doing for money then?" she asked.

Danny, still not sure if he can fully trust her, makes her promise to not judge him or rat him out, mainly not to rat him out. Once she promises not to judge, Danny continues on with telling her how Curt and him have robbed a few places at gunpoint, nothing that has paid out astronomical amounts of cash but that they make enough money where they don't have to do it that often and that Curt is the one who mainly does all the planning for any of their robberies. Sheena sits in silence for a while, simmering in this newfound information that her boyfriend who was just judging her for doing drugs now is telling her that he waves a gun in people's faces till they give them enough money to satisfy him. Then she tells Danny that she wants in. Danny is taken back by this,

"you what?" he asked,

"did I stutter, I said I want in on the robberies. I don't know if you noticed but I don't live in a mansion, in fact, I am behind on rent as it is, so yeah, I could use some extra cash, I want in." she demanded.

With that, the duo gained a third member and this means they will have to do bigger jobs if they wish to make the same money and still split it three ways.

CHAPTER

10

Danny and Sheena reach Danny's apartment. They slowly open the front door and tiptoe to the bedroom to let Curt know that Sheena was the newest member of the gang. Danny was unsure of how Curt would react to the news without giving him a vote. However when Curt was told he was surprisingly thrilled. Having a third person opened up new possibilities and ways to expand. Curt tells them about a potential target he has been eyeing that they should go check out tomorrow.

The morning sun comes up and Danny, Curt, and Sheena head out to see the store Curt has in mind. Curt leads the gang through the town till they reach a pawnshop.

"This is the place." Curt says. The other two not really seeing the potential in it just stare at the building. Curt goes on to explain that it is perfect, a pawnshop of this caliber can not be very organized as far as inventory goes.

There is limitless potential in how much jewelry, gold, silver, and money could be in there. Best of all the store had a subpar lock on the door and Curt has been practicing his lockpicking abilities. So the cheap lock indicates to Curt that the building can't have the best security system in place and the front store window is so full of stuff it blocks any view into the inside. All of this combined makes it a prime target to rob late at night and best of all now that there is a third member they can now afford to have a lookout while both Danny and Curt get the stuff from inside and they can stay inside longer getting more and more valuables. After scooping the place out for about an hour making all the fine-tune adjustments, they head back to the house to get their tools ready to go for that night.

Around midnight Danny meets Sheena on the sidewalk outside of his mom's apartment. Curt goes to retrieve his gun and the few bullets he has as well as his lock picking set, flashlights, and a few duffle bags before also meeting the two outside to once more go over the plan and try to work out any butterflies anyone might have. Once everyone is ready they make their way back to the pawnshop. The neon sign no longer lit up and the inside was pitch black. No cars pass by on the road as they make their way to the door. With ease, Curt gets the door open. Danny and Curt go in while Sheena goes back across the street to be the lookout. The door closes to the store and the two begin to scan the area for the most valuable stuff first. They find the jewelry case in the middle of the store. Curt finds the keyhole to the case and tries to pick it but his cheap pick breaks inside the lock. Seemed the only other option was to smash and grab since they already left evidence behind with the pick. So they begin to smash the glass with their flashlights and snatch up the gold chains, rings, and anything else that shined when the light hit it. Curt then makes his way to the back of the store where the cash register was while Danny cleaned out the remaining jewelry cases. Curt pries open the cash register drawer and pulls out the tray where all the big bills are stored underneath. He starts there, after which he works his way down the tray starting with the twenty-dollar bills. About halfway through the drawer Curt's excitement is through the roof as with every raking motion fills his bag with more money and continues to make it feel heavier and heavier, but then a cold hand grabs his wrist,

"What are you boys doing in here?" says the old store owner as he flips on the lights.

"Hey let go of me!" yells Curt.

"I don't think so, you're a no-good thief and I already have the police on their way!" the old man replies.

Curt looks at Danny while struggling to free his arm from the man's grasp.

"Run!" Curt commands. Danny books it for the door but the old door is stuck shut he fights with it and jiggles the doorknob but it will not budge. Sirens can be heard in the distance getting closer and closer. Danny is now frantic when an explosive boom is heard, leaving his ears ringing. It was Curt, he shot the man. Curt frees his hand from the man who is now bleeding out and runs to Danny as the sirens are getting louder and louder. A desperate act comes over Curt and he shoots another bullet through the front window shattering it, they climb out with just enough time to catch the police cars turning the corner heading for them. They tried to run but Danny was inevitably caught and tackled to the ground. Danny laid there on the cold concrete as the police officer pulled out his handcuffs and began to cuff Danny. He gets one cuff on his wrist before the cop is pushed off Danny and to the ground by Curt. Danny does not know what happened, just that it was an opening to run and that's what he did.

He catches up to Sheena and they run all the way back to Sheena's house.

They spent all night staring out the window filled with paranoia wondering when the door would get kicked in by swat but that time never came. The world seemed to carry on as usual unaware of the events that just transpired. The death of an innocent man had been swallowed up and forgotten about by the world like a ship sinking into the ocean. Worst of all, neither of them know what happened to Curt and the thought of leaving him behind killed a part of Danny. So in a

last-ditch effort to ease his mind, he and
Sheena walk back to Danny's apartment
praying to every deity they could think
of that Curt will be in their room.

They get to the apartment to find
the door is locked. Danny picks up the
welcome mat and takes the spare key,
and unlocks the door and they go inside
yelling for Curt but with no response not
even from Danny's mom. One new
message was on the answering machine.
Danny played the voicemail. It's Curt, he
used his one phone call from jail to call
for Danny's help and Danny wasn't
there. Which made Danny feel even
more guilty about ditching him. Curt
ends the message asking Danny to come
see him at the jail, he learned some news
Danny would be interested in.

CHAPTER

11

Danny and Sheena arrive at the county jail that's holding Curt while he awaits trial. They check-in and are escorted to a glass wall with a phone on each side and hard plastic seats. Curt comes walking in shackled at the wrist and ankles with a guard on his side and sits down on the other side of the glass wall. The click of the phone receiver echoes through Danny's phone. They sit there taking in the moment silently looking at each other.

"How are you?" Danny asked.

"Eh, I've been better." Curt sarcastically responds.

Danny sits there unsure of what to say so he just says nothing. He doesn't know how Curt feels about him running away and ditching him when he got caught saving him. It is a weird state of mind where he has survivor's guilt yet both of them are still alive.

"So, I plan to take a plea deal." Curt says.

"What?" Danny says with shock in his voice.

"Yeah, I killed that man Danny. I already have to deal with that for the rest of my life, but if this plea deal can get me out of prison sooner that is what I want to do." Curt replies.

 "But that's not why I called you, the reason why is your dad Danny."

Danny's eyes widened,

"How is he? How did you get in contact with him?" Danny asked. Curt hesitantly responds,

"Uh well actually Danny, your dad is dead. An old cellmate of his is awaiting trial on a new charge in here and we got to talking. He said your father died not long after arriving at the prison. His cellmate was surprised when I told him you didn't know. He said they usually send a letter."

A disturbed Danny stands silent for a moment, taken back from the sudden news. If there was ever a silver lining to Curt's arrest to Danny, it would be the chance of reconnecting with his father but now that is all gone. And now not only is his only friend behind bars headed for life, but his dad is dead and has been dead and his mother of all people knew yet chose to withhold that from him. Guards come and usher Curt back to his cell. Danny sits quietly for a moment before standing up and rushing out of the prison to go see his mom.

Danny pushes through the door of his mother's apartment. Surprised by the aggressiveness of Danny, his mom peeks out from the kitchen,

"Is everything okay Danny?" she asked.

Danny rubs his hand through the hair on the back of his head as his eyes redden and water fills the lids but no tears fall yet.

"I don't know mom, am I?" He responds.

Danny's mom stands in the room confused by what Danny is trying to hint at.

"Dad's dead!" Danny yells.
"But you already knew that didn't you!"

"What are you talking about?" His mom asked while trying to cover up the truth.

"Don't play dumb with me!" Danny fires back.
"Curt told me everything."

Danny's mom's shoulders drop.

"You were never supposed to find out Danny. Your father was no good, he wasn't worth your time then and he is not worth your time now. Best if you just forget him."

Danny is in disbelief. He scoffs before turning around and leaving the apartment, exiting with a thunderous slam of the front door behind him. Sheena stands outside waiting for Danny before they set off back to Sheena's apartment. Danny, filled with rage, says nothing as to not say anything that might hurt Sheena by accident and Sheena remains silent because she is unsure of how to comfort Danny.

Back at Sheena's apartment the two lay down on the couch. Danny lays his head on Sheena's stomach and Sheena plays with Danny's hair. Hours turn into seconds and before long it is midnight. Finally, Danny feels as though he has cooled off enough to begin talking. Without moving to look at Sheena he starts to let it all out, not just about what took place earlier that day but all of the problems he had been bottling up over the years. When he was finished and a trail of tears running down his cheek, Sheena stops rubbing his head. She has Danny sit up before asking him,

"Do you wanna do something that will make you forget all of the pain?"

Sheena goes off and retrieves a box and then places it on the coffee table in front of Danny and flips it open. Inside is an unorganized supply of syringes, a spoon, and a bag of cloudy white crystal shards.

Sheena takes Danny's arm and ties it with surgical tubing then takes some of the crystals out and smashes them with the spoon, she then scoops them up in the spoon and liquefies them, taking one of the syringes she sucks up the liquid and slowly begins to bring the syringe closer to Danny's arm. Danny is no longer thinking about his father or his mom, he now has a look of fear on his face, unsure of what is about to happen. Sheena smiles and tells him to

"Just relax."

Before she pushes the end of the needle into Danny's vein. She pushes the plunger down, sending the liquid into his body before untying the tube from his arm. Quickly, Danny is met with an overwhelming feeling of euphoria that is then followed by an unbelievable rush of energy and his perception of himself seemed to be superhuman to him at the time. He felt like he could hear his heart beating in his ears and pounding against his ribs. Sheena was right, it did take away all of Danny's pain, and just like that, he was addicted. Danny felt like he was entering a new chapter of life and he didn't care what life threw at him as long as he had two things, Sheena and meth.

CHAPTER

12

Now that Sheena is the only person left in Danny's life he cares about, he wants to give her the best that he has to offer. One day while they are both sitting around the empty apartment Danny brings up that he actually likes her apartment but he doesn't feel like it is where he belongs. He tells Sheena he wants a place he feels he can call home. Sheena begins to think maybe Danny is leaving her but all worries are washed away when Danny proposes the idea of the two of them getting out of the apartment and going out and buying a house. Instead of being renters they should be homeowners. Sheena finds it hard to continue to portray the hard punk girl image she always strives to have when Danny brings up buying a house with her. The little girl in her comes out as she smiles and a small high-pitched squeal can be heard.

"Really? You mean it?" Sheena asked with excitement.

"Yeah I am serious, we should go looking around to see if we can find anything we like that we could afford." Danny responds.

Danny looks at the clock.

"You know, we still have a good amount of daylight left, if you hurry to get your jacket we might have enough time to go looking around the town."

The two of them set off around town, they only stick to the impoverished areas because as much as they would like to shoot for the stars, they know their own limitations and would rather not get their hopes up. They are already looking at houses out of what they can afford for two people that do not have any money. They eventually find a house they like, it is a single-family home with a small overgrown yard. The house itself is falling apart but the skeleton of it seems to be intact. Some would say it's a good symbolism for Danny himself, falling apart on the outside but still standing strong. Those people are wrong, it's just a house. But it could soon be their house. Now all they need to do is come up with the money. Sheena brings up that her uncle works at a bank and he might be able to help them get a loan. The two take one last gitty look at the house before turning around and heading to the bank.

They reach the impressive concrete building that is the bank that Sheena's uncle works at. They walk in through the double glass doors that are trimmed in gold and are welcomed with a row of tellers and lines clogging each desk. Sheena's uncle works from another desk and in the middle of the phone call he was having he looked up to see his niece

"yeah, uh-huh, okay I got to go!" Her uncle says rushing through his call. "That can't be Sheena is it?" Her uncle says from across the room with a plastic smile.

Sheena and Danny look over to see a man in an ill-fitting gray suit with a thick mustache and dark hair that is balding, standing up from his desk.

"Hey, Uncle Robert!" Sheena responds as they both head toward each other with their arms wide open before meeting with an embrace.

Letting go of each other, Sheena's uncle holds her by the shoulders.

"What are you doing here?" Her uncle asked.

"We are looking to buy a house and were wanting to know if we could get a loan." Sheena replies.

A shocked look on her uncle's face, he leads them over to his desk.

"So you are wanting to buy a house? Do you have a bank account here?" He asked.

The two look at each other,

"No." Sheena answers.

"Well do you have any credit?" He asked.

Danny and Sheena look down.

"No, we don't," Sheena replies again as she feels the world crumbling with the feeling of not being qualified for any loan.

"Have you quit the drugs?" He asked.

"Yeah, I have been clean for six months now." Sheena replies.

"That's good, do you have a job?"

"Yeah, I do have a job actually." Uncle Robert leans back in his chair, his tucked-in dress shirt stretching to the max before reforming back to its original shape when he comes forward, his hands pressed against each other like he was praying.

"Listen, you really do not meet any of the qualifications to be approved for a loan, but since it seems you are trying to clean up your life I think we can take a chance on you. So I will go ahead and approve you now."

Both Sheena and Danny smile with excitement bursting from the seams, they can not seem to think Uncle Robert enough before leaving to go and get the house of their dreams.

As time goes on they make small improvements to the house with what little money they have. But honestly most of the money they manage to gather is usually spent on drugs. Which works out because they don't bother making payments to the bank for the loan anyways and the stack of letters from the bank that are piling up on the counter and their landline's answering machine being completely filled with voicemails from Uncle Robert shows for it. One morning though Danny wakes up and stumbles into the living room and there on the ground at the foot of the front door was another letter from the bank but not like the others that came before it. This one was different, "Notice Of Foreclosure" in big bold lettering. For the first time the bank had scared Danny. He shakes Sheena awake waving the letter in her face,

"We got to get ahold of your uncle, he has to fix this." Danny says.

Sheena hops out of bed, they both rush to get dressed and speed down to the bank. Inside is the same old scene, tellers at their desk with lines of people in front of each one. Quiet conversations are heard from each of the tellers as they try their best to assist their clients. The only thing missing is Uncle Robert. They walk over to the other loan officer to ask where he is.

"Today is his day off." the loan officer tells them.

"Well I'm his niece and I need to talk to him, it's important, can you have him call me when he gets back in?" Sheena asked.

The loan officer agreed and that was all they could do. Now, whatever happens is out of their control. Sheena had not had any real contact with her uncle for years so she doesn't know where he lives, she doesn't know his home phone number, all she knew was that he worked at that bank last time she saw him and hoped he still worked there when they needed the loan. They go back home to relax and take their minds off this new situation they had found themselves in by the most popular pastime in the house, drugs. That's what they did. For hours they sat around shooting up and smoking cigarettes till they were all out of cigarettes. Danny tried to tip over the pack as if magically one last cigarette would fall out but when one didn't he threw the pack to the side and went to get his jacket,

"I guess I'll go get more." Danny says.

"What? Can't you wait till the morning?" asked Sheena.

"I'm just going right down the street, it will only be ten minutes max, just chill out here and I'll be back soon." Danny replied already with his jacket on walking out the door.

Danny felt like a zoo animal that just broke free from his cage and now is left to wonder. He had never been high and in public like this before. He goes down the steps of the porch and onto the sidewalk and continues on the path till he is greeted by the bright convenience store lights and the bell ringing as he opens the door. He asks the clerk for three packs of his favorite brand of cigarettes, the clerk without thinking, runs through the motions of retrieving the cigarettes but they only had one pack left. The clerk then offered him the one pack or Danny could get a carton of them, Danny went with the carton. The clerk rang it up and Danny handed him a handful of balled-up dollar bills that had been stuffed in his pocket and just as the bell welcomed him when he walked in, it also told of a sweet goodbye when he left.

Danny retraces his steps back to the house not looking up from his feet so as to not draw any suspicion to him. He opens the front door to the house,

"Hey!" Danny shouts as he comes back home,

"They didn't have three packs, so I just got us a carton." He announces.

"Sheena?" he calls out but no answer.

"Sheena, where are you?" he tries to call out again. He begins to investigate every room till he comes to the bathroom. The door was shut but water could be heard pouring from the bathtub.

"Hey Sheena!" he yells through the door,

"They didn't have three packs," Danny says as he opens the door to the bathroom only to find the bathroom floor flooded and the tub overflowing.

Sheena's pale body laying in the tub with her arms on either side. Danny walks in, turns off the faucet, and looks closer at Sheena. She was dead. The foam was still present on the side of her mouth, her lifeless body just staring off into the abyss. Danny drains the tub and wraps a towel around her leaving her in the tub before calling for an ambulance. Danny sits on the toilet seat smoking one of the cigarettes he just bought while watching the EMTs lift Sheena's corpse onto a gurney and transport her out the door.

CHAPTER

13

Miserably, Danny stands up by the casket in the funeral home as a small crowd of people usher themselves in. The room had been set up to hold close to one hundred people, most of the seats however were empty. One by one the line of people would walk through and look into the casket where Sheena's lifeless body lay. Then they would move on to Danny, shaking his hand or giving him a hug followed by some cheesy line like "she looks so natural." or "she is no longer suffering." Danny would just nod and agree with these strangers.

Uncle Robert could be found in the middle of the line and he came up and looked into the coffin. Then, like all of those who came before him, he met Danny. He hugged him and told him what a shame it was and that he couldn't imagine losing someone so close to him. With his hands still on each of Danny's shoulders, he proceeded to ask when and if Danny had any intentions of paying off the loan. At that moment Danny couldn't stand to look him in the eyes. Tears of anger begin to form around Danny's eyes, and his fists become clenched.

"Yeah, I'll be paying you back, don't worry about it." Danny tells him.

"Good." Uncle Robert replies while patting Danny's shoulder before finding a seat. Danny becomes filled with rage over the interaction. His leg begins to shake and Danny's hearing fades away to the point where the preacher, who is now talking at the podium, sounds like he is underwater. Danny silently interrupts the service by showing himself to the restroom to cool off.

Danny loses it in the bathroom and punches the mirror shattering it to pieces and cutting his hand in the process and for the first time since Sheena's death, Danny could feel again. So Danny picks up a piece of the broken glass, rolls up his sleeve, and slowly drags the shard across his skin. Deep maroon blood rushes out from the cut and Danny takes a sigh of relief. The distant voice of the preacher could still be heard coming from the other room but Danny decides he couldn't stand to be there any longer with Robert. While everyone is busy listening to people tell stories about their time with Sheena, he makes a break for the door and when the fresh air hits his face he could no longer hold back the tears. He tries to not cry but can not control it. He wipes his eyes with his hands leaving behind a faded red splotch of blood on his face. He gets back to his house and frantically walks inside while cursing under his breath. He makes his way over to the couch where Sheena kept her box and he pulls it out. When he flips the box open he finds all of the usual stuff, the bag of crystals, surgical tubing, spoon, lighter, syringes.

He begins to concoct his recipe to forget his pain. Tying the surgical tube to himself and slapping the bend of his arm to get his veins to raise. Danny slams the biggest dose he had done in his life. His goal was to not wake up and to just die without pain. Eventually, the small leftover amount of crystals he had was all used up. This only fueled Danny's anger more. He took the box and dumped it upside down. He had himself believing there had to be more, that could not have been all of it.

There was no more meth in the box, instead, Danny found Curt's gun that Sheena had taken from him on that robbery gone wrong. This gun calmed him down. He also found the bullets on the floor and put them into the magazine followed by racking one into the chamber. This gave Danny what he believed to be the best idgea of his life. Danny could not sleep at all that night. Whether it was the idea he had planted in his own head or the high quantity of meth swimming through his bloodstream is anyone's guess, but all I know is Danny was up to greet the sun the following morning.

He throws on his leather jacket, walks over to the counter and grabs all those letters from the bank, and then heads out of the front door to solve his financial issue. Once again standing outside of the massive concrete bank building, Danny is welcomed in by the door greeter. He tries to not make eye contact as he gets in line for the nearest bank teller. While he is waiting, Uncle Robert notices Danny and tries to get his attention. Danny, unable to keep from looking in his direction, does nothing but reluctantly wave to him before going back to staring at the ground. He continues to wait impatiently in the long line, he can't seem to stand still. About an hour passed before the line had shrunk down to it being Danny's turn.

He is met by a young blonde lady who had a very kind voice and asked Danny how she could help him.

"You can hand over all the money." Danny mumbles not even looking at her.

"I'm sorry what?" the bank teller asked with a smile still on her face.

Danny then pulls the pistol out from his jacket pointing it at the teller,

"I said hand over all of the money!" Danny yells.

The bank becomes a frenzy of people running for their lives. The lady behind the desk hands over all the money she can throw at him and Danny snatches it all up. He stands up on the desk and walks down the row gathering all of the money from every bank teller. He then hops down and walks over to Uncle Robert's desk where he is on the phone begging for cops to come quickly.

Danny drops all of the bank's letters onto his desk along with all of the money he just stole from the front.

"Here is your money!" Danny yells.

"Here take it, it's so important to you right?" Danny says with a crazed look on his face.

He then lifts the pistol up and with a deep breath pumps Uncle Roberts' chest with three bullets. Danny exhales and sirens are seen arriving at the front door. He had no choice but to go up the stairs. The Swat team takes formation and begins clearing the first level of the bank and collectively moving up to the next floor. Meanwhile, a crowd of onlookers gather outside and local journalists show up. Danny had come to a dead-end. He found himself on the roof with nowhere left to run. After everything Danny had done he knew he was caught. He sits down patiently on the ledge of the skyscraping bank waiting for the cops to come and take him away. The swat team swarmed up the stairs to the roof,

"Let me see some hands!" they all shouted with their rifles drawn.

Danny sits there motionless while the blades of the helicopter above could be heard slicing through the air. The swat gets closer still pointing their guns. A deafening bang and a splash of red mist rain down from Danny's skull as he plummets to Earth. Danny Collins was without a doubt dead.

Even though I hadn't put on the badge in years, that day will forever live inside my head. I saw plenty of things while on the force, but nothing like that day on the roof, nothing like the case of Danny Collins.